Stinson Beach Children's Holiday
E May
Rudolph, the red-nosed reindeer,
31111036777843

W9-BZY-211

Library Measure Funds
Thank You Marin County Voters!

THIS BOOK BELONGS TO

_____

_____

LITTLE SIMON

An imprint of Simon & Schuster Children's Publishing Division
1230 Avenue of the Americas, New York, New York 10020
First Little Simon hardcover edition September 2015
Rudolph Shines Again published by permission of Pearson Education, Inc. Text copyright © 2003 by Robert L. May
Illustrations copyright © 2015 by Antonio Javier Caparo
All rights reserved, including the right of reproduction in whole or in part in any form.
LITTLE SIMON is a registered trademark of Simon & Schuster, Inc., and associated colophon is a trademark of Simon & Schuster, Inc.
For information about special discounts for bulk purchases, please contact Simon & Schuster Special Sales at 1-866-506-1949 or
business@simonandschuster.com. The Simon & Schuster Speakers Bureau can bring authors to your live event. For more information
or to book an event contact the Simon & Schuster Speakers Bureau at 1-866-248-3049 or visit our website at www.simonspeakers.com.
Designed by Angela Navarra and Chani Yammer
Manufactured in China 0715 SCP
10 9 8 7 6 5 4 3 2 1
Library of Congress Cataloging-in-Publication Data
May, Robert Lewis, 1905-1976
[Rudolph, the red-nosed reindeer, shines again]
Rudolph shines again / by Robert L. May ; illustrated by Antonio Javier Caparo. —
First Little Simon edition. pages cm
Originally published by Maxton in 1954 under title:
Rudolph, the red-nosed reindeer, shines again.
Summary: Devastated when his nose no longer shines brightly,
Rudolph spends his time worrying, weeping, and feeling sorry for
himself until he searches for two baby rabbits lost in the woods.
ISBN 978-1-4424-7498-7 (hardcover : alk. paper) — ISBN 978-1-4424-7499-4 (eBook)
[1. Stories in rhyme. 2. Reindeer—Fiction. 3. Christmas—Fiction.]
I. Caparo, Antonio Javier, illustrator. II. Title.
PZ8.3.M4525Rr 2015
[E]—dc23
2013045128

RUDOLPH
SHINES AGAIN

By Robert L. May   Illustrated by Antonio Javier Caparo

LITTLE SIMON

New York   London   Toronto   Sydney   New Delhi

'Twas a month before Christmas, when Rudolph, at play,
Saw Santa drive up, to call from his sleigh,

"The weatherman says there'll be snow Christmas Eve.
So please tell your parents I'd like you to leave,

To lead all my deer through that dark, snowy night,
With your shining red nose and its wonderful light.

Meanwhile, of course, you can work on the toys
We'll be taking, this Christmas, to good girls and boys."

As Rudolph was hitched up in front of the rest,
He heard the deer whisper, "What makes him the best?"

"We're bigger and stronger!" "And older!" "You said it!"
"But we get the backaches, while he gets the credit!"

The deer in the workshop were mean to him too.
They gave him the messiest gluing to do.

He carried the heaviest loads of them all.
And when football was played, they made Rudolph the ball!

Poor Rudolph! He worried, he wept, and he whined.
And the more he shed tears, the less his nose shined!

"Oh, poor little me," he would pity and pout,
Till one day the light in his nose just went out!

"With *this* nose, I never could lead Santa's sleigh!
I'm useless here now, so why should I stay?"

"I'll leave here tonight while the rest are in bed,
And go to some faraway country instead,

Where none of the new folks who'll be introduced to me
Know how much brighter my nose really used to be!"

He left and he traveled, for mile after mile,
Till one day, when ready to rest for a while,

In a field with a very thick forest behind it,
He heard a strange noise! But he just couldn't find it

Until he came close, for darkness was falling.
Hundreds of rabbits were crying and calling,

"Two of our children, Donnie and Doris,
 Taking a walk, got lost in the forest!"

"It's much, much too dark now to search or to follow them!"
"By morning, a fox or a wolf will have swallowed them!"

"If only we rabbits had eyes like a cat!"
"Or a bright shining flashlight, we sure could use that!"

Thought Rudolph, "These rabbits have *reason* to worry!
I'd better stop pitying *me* in a hurry!"

And right then and there, Rudolph ended his habits
Of pouting and tears, and thought just of the rabbits.

"I'll find them," he shouted. "I'll find Donnie and Doris
With my bright shining nose!" And he dashed for the forest!

Completely forgetting himself and his woes,
He'd even forgotten the change in his nose!

Because he was running as fast as he could,
When he learned his mistake, he was deep in the wood!

He now faced the risks of that dangerous place
With a nose no more bright than the one on *your* face!

"I promised the rabbits their babies I'd save.
I may have been stupid; I've got to be brave!

My nose doesn't shine, but like all the other deers',
It's still a good sniffer; I still have sharp ears."

Quickly and quietly, he ran through the forest,
Sniffing and listening for Donnie and Doris.

(And sniffing and listening, too, for the sly
Foxes and wolves that he knew were close by.)

With all that huge forest to search without light,
Do you think that Rudolph will find them that night?

Perhaps it was smartness, perhaps it was luck.
Or perhaps a reward for his bravery and pluck

Was sent by an angel, from way, way up high,
Who steered Rudolph's feet toward a very small cry

From a thick patch of bushes. And that's where he found them,
Frightened, but safe, with leaves piled around them

To keep out the cold, and wild animals, too.
"I'm your friend," Rudolph whispered. "I've come here for you,

To help you get home. So please, have no fears!
Just jump on my back, and hold tight to my ears.

The foxes and wolves here would all like to meet us,
In order to cook us, and carve us, and eat us!"

So Rudolph bent down, and the bunnies obeyed.
He then ran so fast that no animal laid

A claw or a tooth on the bunnies or deer.
(Though two panting wolves came just terribly near!)

Then out of the woods, for a grand, happy landing
In the field where the crowd of sad rabbits were standing.

Just picture the Mother and Dad Rabbits' joy,
When Rudolph brought back both their girl and their boy!

They thanked him and thanked him, and begged him to stay.
Said Rudolph, "I'll come for a visit some day.

But my job is with Santa, to help as I can.
I was wrong to go 'way from that wonderful man.

Perhaps it was 'cause of my weeping and whining
That all of a sudden my nose stopped its shining!

With a dull nose, last night in the woods, I helped *you*.
In that case, I surely could help Santa, too!

As Santa's front reindeer, I guess I'm all through.
But I still could load boxes, or work with the glue."

As tears from the rabbits' eyes started to roll,
He started his trip to the far-off North Pole.

Before this remarkable journey was through,
'Twas the day before Christmas! And darker it grew.

The gray northern sky and the fog and the snow
Would make almost anyone travel quite slow,

Or even get lost! But Rudolph just flew
Straight as an arrow, and speedily, too,

Through the heaviest snowstorm and fog of the season!
How did he do it? Can you guess the reason?

Ever since Rudolph had saved the young rabbits,
Forgetting himself, and ended his habits

Of thinking of Rudolph, and weeping and whining,
The light on his nose had again started shining!

At first very little, too dimly to view with it.
(Do you think that the angel had something to do with it?)

Then slowly more bright, like a red glowing coal,
Until, when at last he could see the North Pole

And Santa's big sleigh by the workshop front door,
It shone just as brightly as ever before!

The deer were all hitched, the sleigh almost loaded,
And Santa so worried, he nearly exploded.

"Without Rudolph's red nose and its wonderful glow,
How will I steer through the fog and the snow?"

But when he saw Rudolph, he shouted, "Hurray!
Quick, take your place at the head of the sleigh!"

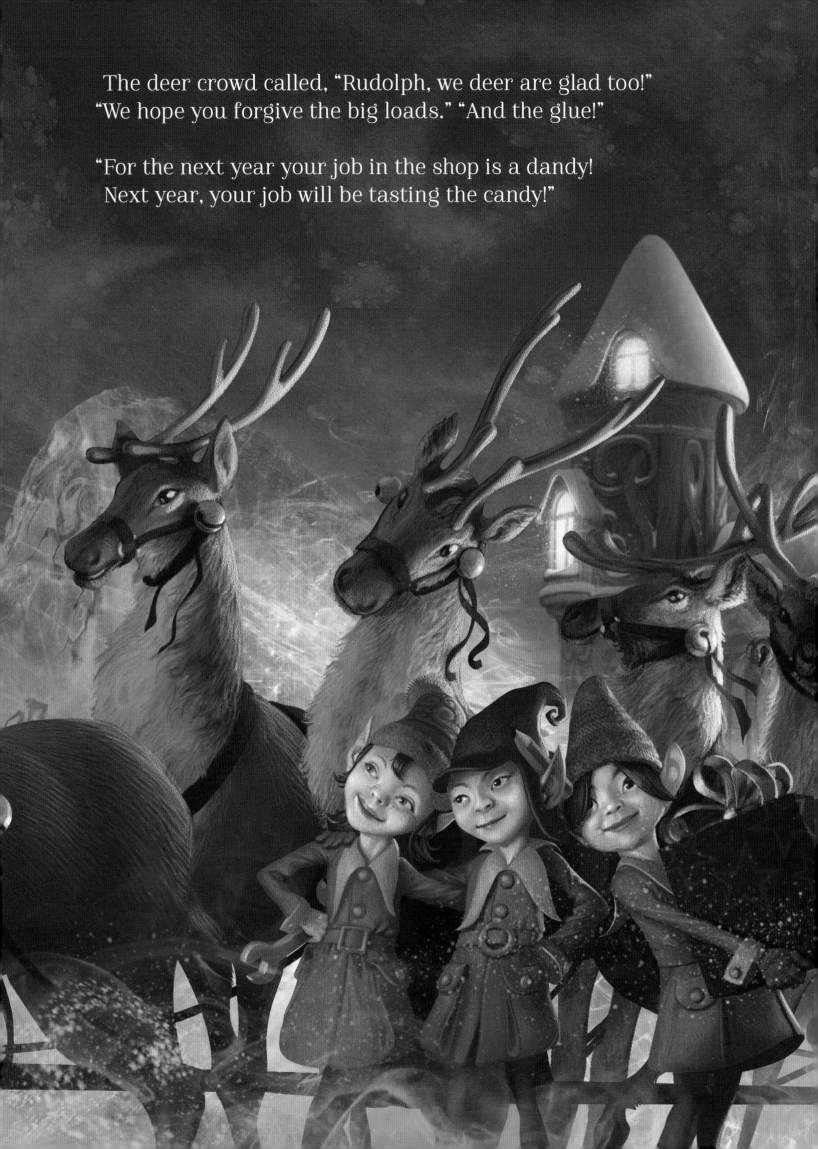

The deer crowd called, "Rudolph, we deer are glad too!"
"We hope you forgive the big loads." "And the glue!"

"For the next year your job in the shop is a dandy!
Next year, your job will be tasting the candy!"

So happy young Rudolph led Santa's great sleigh,
With Rudolph's red nose again lighting the way

Through darkness and fog, to deliver the toys
That were given that Christmas to good girls and boys.

Swiftly they traveled, as Rudolph's nose shone
On each waiting chimney, including your own!

The very first sound you could hear on the roof
As Santa's sleigh landed was Rudolph's small hoof.

Then his nose made the light that gave Santa a view
Of you and your room. And when they were through . . .

You might, too, have heard, as they drove out of sight,

"Merry Christmas to all,
and to all a good night!"